Dragonory

And other stories for 7-9 year olds

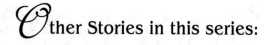

Dragonory

And other stories for 7-9 year olds

Compiled by
PIE CORBETT

To all those parents, storytellers and teachers who keep the flame of stories alive in children's minds.

To Edmund - more stories for your golden box.

Introduction © 2008, Pie Corbett
© 2008 Scholastic Ltd
Illustrations © Lisa Berkshire
Designed using Adobe InDesign

Published by Scholastic Ltd
Villiers House
Clarendon Avenue
Leamington Spa
Warwickshire
CV32 5PR
www.scholastic.co.uk

Printed in the UK by CPI Bookmarque

1 2 3 4 5 6 7 8 9   8 9 0 1 2 3 4 5 6 7

British Library Cataloguing-in-Publication Data
A catalogue record for this book is available from the British Library.

ISBN 978-1407-10065-4

Acknowledgements

Every effort has been made to trace copyright holders for the works reproduced in this book, and the publishers apologise for any inadvertent omissions.
Pie Corbett for the use of *Tattercoats, The Papaya that Spoke, The Old Man and the Donkey, Mulenga and the Cherries*, and *Lazy Jack* retold bt Pie Corbett © 2008, Pie Corbett (2008, previously unpublished).
Helen East for the use of *Spider's Wife* retold by Helen East © 2008, Helen East (2008, previously unpublished).
Joseph Jacobs for the use of *Master of all Masters* retold by Joesph Jacobs © 2008, Joseph Jacobs (2008, previously unpublished).
Jackie Andrews for the use of *Little Leo and the Moon Rabbit* retold by Jackie Andrews © 2008, Jackie Andrews (2008, previously unpublished).
Usha Bahl for the use of *Matiwara's Name Game* retold by Usha Bahl from 'Scholastic Collections: Tales Myths and Legenends' compiled by Pie Corbett © 1993, Usha Bahl (1993, Scholastic Limited).
Helen Frances for the use of *The Liar* retold by Helen Frances © 2008, Helen Frances (2008, previously unpublished).
Jane Grell for the use of *Bimwili and the Zimwi* by Jane Grell © 2008, Jane Grell (2008, previously unpublished).
Xanthe Gresham for the use of *Awongaleema* retold by Xanthe Gresham © 2008, Xanthe Gresham (2008, previously unpublished).
Daniel Morden for the use of *The Monster Over the Hill* retold by Daniel Morden © 2008, Daniel Morden (2008, previously unpublished).
Andrew Fusek Peters for the use of *Jack Foretells the Future* retold by Andrew Fusek Peters © 2008, Andrew Fusek Peters (2008, previously unpublished).
Jess Smith for the use of *Dragonory* retold by Jess Smith© 2008, Jess Smith (2008, previously unpublished).
Taffy Thomas for the use of *The Clever Wish* and *The Snapdragon Plant* both retold by Taffy Thomas © 2008, Taffy Thomas (2008, previously unpublished).
The publishers would like to thank Xanthe Gresham, Pie Corbett and Taffy Thomas for their readings on the audio CD and also Linden Studios and Adrian Moss for the audio CD development.

Contents

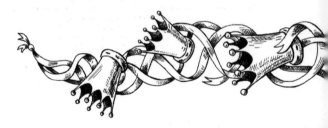

$\mathcal{C}$ontents continued

Introduction

Three golden apples fall from heaven –
one is for the person who tells the tale;
one is for the person who listens;
and one is for the person who passes it on.

Storytelling weaves a spell that binds us all into one world community. We enter that other world where anything is possible and we can think, feel and grow together. Stories help sustain and create our community. They help to fashion who we are and to know what is right and what is wrong. Stories cherish the human spirit within ourselves and within the children who listen to and tell them.

All cultures have songs, art, dance, religion – and of course, stories. Without the stories of our culture, we have no culture.

Research has shown that children who are read to and hear stories before going to school are the most likely to succeed in school. This is because stories help children to sit still, listen and concentrate; they also help to develop abstract thinking so that children who have had stories told or read to them are the first to form abstract concepts across the curriculum. In addition, stories create a comforting imaginative world in which ogres can be confronted and our deepest fears played out and controlled.

It is worth noticing how the most proficient writers in any class are readers. They are children who were probably read to before they went to school, have a bedtime story every night and have become avid readers themselves. This constant repetition of listening to and reading stories has helped them internalise the patterns they need to create stories of their own. Because you cannot create stories out of nothing.

Pie Corbett 2008

The Clever Wish

Retold by Taffy Thomas

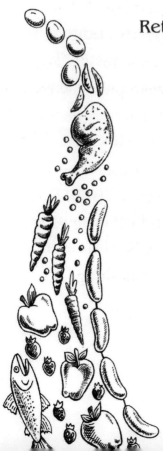

There was once a man and he was desperately unlucky: he had no food and no money. And as if that wasn't bad enough, he had a wife who was desperate to have a baby. No matter how hard they tried, they couldn't have a baby. So he had no food, no money and no baby.

And as if that wasn't bad enough, he had a mother who was completely blind. So he had no food, no money, no baby and a blind mother.

What could he do? He thought the least he could do was feed them. So he borrowed a gun and went off to the woods to shoot a rabbit. He thought he could make rabbit stew, and although rabbit stew is not a great dinner, it is better than no dinner at all.

He was just looking for a rabbit to shoot when there was a flash of white, and he parted the bushes. And there in the bush, with its hoof stuck in a trap, was a unicorn – a snow-white horse with one golden spiral horn – and he thought, "Yum, yum, unicorn stew."

So he put his gun to the unicorn's head and he was just about to pull the trigger when the unicorn spoke to him.

The unicorn said, "Now listen, I'm a magical creature. If you spare my life, I can give you one magic wish."

He thought, "Money!" and he put his gun down and took the unicorn out of the trap. The unicorn looked him straight in the eye and said, "Now listen, money is not the answer to everything and you have only got one wish, so use it wisely."

And if his first thought was for money, his second thought was for food, but his third thought was for a baby, and his fourth thought was for his mother's eyesight to be healed.

So you see, that is the dilemma of this story. He has only got one wish. So what does he wish for?

Anyway, the story is called The Clever Wish so I will tell you the wish that he made. He thought very hard, then he wished that his mother could see him and his wife rocking their baby in a golden cradle.

And as he made that wish, there was

a flash of blue light and he and his wife
were rocking a golden cradle with a
newborn baby in it, and his mother was
stood at the end of the cradle, smiling
and waving because she could see.

But of course a baby doesn't need a
golden cradle, so that very afternoon
they sold it. With the money they got for
the cradle, they bought enough food to

feed the whole family for many, many months.

Now they were all happy, so are we.

So put on the kettle… we'll have a cup of tea.

Jack Foretells The Future

Retold by Andrew
Fusek Peters

Jack's ears perked up when he heard the sound of sawing. In the trees not far off, he saw a farmer cutting a branch. The only problem was that the farmer was standing on the branch he was sawing.

"Excuse me, Mr Farmer, I couldn't help but notice – "

"Push off, little brat!" shouted the

farmer. "Can't you see I am busy?"

"But, Mr Farmer!" said Jack. "You're going to fall off the tree!"

"Oh, am I indeed?" said the farmer, who had not twigged what was about to happen. "And you, no doubt, can tell the future! Well, some of us have work to do. Now go on, shove off!"

With that, the farmer, who was a few leaves short of a bush, carried on sawing. As Jack made his merry way, he heard a resounding *crash!* Jack rushed back to see the farmer piled in a heap on the ground. He helped the farmer up and the old man took his hat off to Jack.

"Amazing. Incredible. In front of my very eyes, this boy foretold the future!" The farmer was very excited.

Jack was not too sure how to answer. "It was nothing!" he said modestly.

The farmer reached into his pocket and pulled out a bag of gold coins.

"My boy," he exclaimed, "this bag will be yours if you can tell me when I am going to die!"

Jack was nonplussed. He had no idea. The farmer was not very bright, but the gold certainly was, as it gleamed in the summer sunlight.

By the tree, the farmer's donkey was standing quietly in the shade having a little snooze. Jack was inspired.

"Mr Farmer," he yammered and stammered, "only when your donkey sneezes three times will you finally depart this life!"

"Oh, magnificent! Miraculous!" sang the farmer. "My donkey has never had an ill day in all his long and lazy life."

The gold was handed over, hands were shook and Jack went off on a shopping spree.

As for the farmer, well, as he saddled up the donkey on a summery day full of bees and breezes and pollen, the donkey's nose stirred and squirmed and suddenly exploded, *"Atchooooo!"*

"Oh, my Lord!" wailed the farmer. "The first time he's sneezed in twenty years! What shall I do?"

He quickly put a feedbag over the donkey's nose.

"No nasty pollen will get you now, my dear nag!" said the farmer. But the material was scratchy. Donkey's nose shivered and shook. And a few seconds later came a shocking, "*Atchooooo!*"

"Oh! Oh! Oh, my dear Lord!" cried the farmer. "The second time he's sneezed in twenty years! What can I do?" He had a bright idea! He saw two round pebbles on the ground. He picked them up and stuffed them up the donkey's nostrils.

"Now I'll be safe!" said the farmer. "I'll live to a ripe old age, yes I shall. Yes I shall!"

Unfortunately, those pebbles did not make the donkey happy. Oh, how they irritated him. His nose was very uncomfortable and itchy. The itch grew larger and larger. Donkey's nose bustled and blustered and finally burst with an, "*Atchooooo!*"

The first pebble shot from his nose like a bullet and hit the farmer on one

side of his head. The second pebble flew
from his nostrils like an arrow and hit
the farmer on the other side of the head,
and the farmer promptly fell down.

Dead.

Dragonory

Retold by Jess Smith

Long ago in summertime, when I was a small child living on the road as a traveller child, it would always be the practice in the evening – after our outside fire was flamed and food eaten – for all the children to sit around a big campfire and listen to our favourite traveller tales.

Old Uncle William was our storyteller; although he never referred to himself as a normal teller of tales. He said when we called him king of the tellers – that "he wasn't a man or a woman, not black nor white or any colour in between. He wasn't old or young, nor was he a dog or a cat, a bird or a fish."

He would also laugh and say that he was invisible and needed to wear a bright multicoloured coat so folks would see him coming and know that if children behaved they were in for a real treat.

"So, kids, what am I?" he would ask us as we sat wide-eyed, wondering what kind of creature he was about to be, especially for us. "What am I, kids?"

he'd laugh and call out so that every child in the green would gather round. Altogether we'd shout as loud as we could, "You're old Dragonory, so tell us a story."

Old Uncle William has been dead a long time now, but I never forgot how he told his tales. So if you lend me your ears and give me a little of your time I shall share some of them with you.

Dragons don't come about nowadays – don't seem any call for them I suppose, with them being extinct and all that stuff. Shame that, because they make wonderful storytellers. Yes! Honest!

You see, in times that were neither here nor there, when rivers ran uphill and birds flew backwards, dragons ruled the land. Great heaving brutes with red eyes and green scaly wings would glide over the land watching and seeing everything. Nobody liked them.

You wouldn't either if there was always the chance your back end might get flamed by their fiery breath – if they happened to skid land behind you on the ground, that is, if you lived away back in them times, that is, of course!

Do you know that dragons told tales of witches and fairies and bogey goblins and jaggy hedgehogs and shiny feathered crows and many creatures big and small?

Now, no one knows why, but after months of heavy rain, the old ones said the dragons were seen less and less, and they thought the dragons were allergic to water.

A shame that, because, as I said, they were brilliant storytellers.

What's that you say? You'd like to know more about dragons? Well, don't tell a living soul but I happen to know where one lives. Yes, hand over heart, it's positively true – a real live dragon. He's not as big as those other ones, or as scaly, and his breath, well it's more of a hiss than a flame, but I think if we ask him

I'm sure he'd tell us some tales.

"How can we do that?" I hear you ask in unison. Well, at your age it's possible to think mystic and magic. You can sing with birds and speak to hamsters. So while you are still a young person, let's go and call on Dragonory, the story dragon.

Close eyes now – come on, no peeking! Are those eyes tightly closed? Good. Now if you are relaxed, think dragon, dragon! Can you see him? Isn't he small? Same size as you! And see, no hot flaming tongue or deep red eyes – just a small, slightly green sort of... frog-like, lizard-ish, smiling-faced creature.

"Hello there, Dragonory. Some young people to hear stories."

Now sit back and he'll tell you how his storytelling began.

"Hi there, guys and dolls. Nice to meet you.

"Well, it all began after the dragons disappeared. I was terrified, me being so helpless and small, but hey, I couldn't let the people know that or they'd not take dragon roars seriously. And as I was the last dragon, it was important to frighten people. So I built a woody bridge over a fast-flowing river and as people tried to cross I would roar out loud. I would laugh as they scuppered away from my bridge.

"To cross, those scaredy-custard people had to pay me money. And I had a big bag of gold. And my bag got bigger, and so did my power.

"But one day a boy came along and said, 'I need to go over the bridge because my granny is sick in her bed and my mum has packed a basket with fruit and sandwiches for her.'

"I told this silly boy if he wanted so bad to cross the river he needed money, lots and lots of money.

"'Hello,' he said, 'I'm called Toki.

What is your name, and why do you want money?'

"I told Toki I didn't tell people my name because I was the fearsome dragon and he had to give me money – no money, no crossing. He just stared at me, that Toki boy, didn't even flinch a muscle, not even when I stared my big, beautiful, red eyes at his tiny blue ones.

"He must have been a very brave boy, he just stared right back. He's mad, I thought. He has to be – anyone else would have run off. I felt sorry for this Toki and thought I'd try him with a riddle. I knew he'd never get the answers in a million, trillion years. People are stupid, dragons are wise.

"So I said to this Toki fellow, 'Three riddles for you, my lad, and a hundred golden pieces for each wrong answer you give me.' I knew he'd never get the right ones – answers, that is.

"'Go on then Dragon, I'm not afraid of you or your riddles. My teacher told me I'm the cleverest in my school, so bring them on.'

"So with my green-and-red thinking brain working harder than ever, I said, 'OK, how many stars in the night heavens? Yes, think on that clever Toki fella. Number two: who is the bravest, fiercest creature in this upside-down world?'

"Ha, I could see him getting this silly look on his face, I knew he was stumped. 'Number three is the hardest of all: what am I thinking? Now go home to wherever you come from and don't bother me again.'

"Toki fella didn't go away. Instead he stared me right in the eye and said, 'I'll take some time but if you leave me in peace for an hour or so and keep your stupid mouth closed, I'll work out the

answers. But if I get them right, that means you will have to leave this bridge free for everyone to use.'

"I was mighty angry with this Toki fella, so I rose up my scaly spine and shook my tail and knocked him so hard he went flat on the ground. 'Now, will you go away?' I asked him.

"He was braver than I first thought because he dusted off his trousers and sat down. He said I was taking advantage and not playing fair. He said I was a nasty dragon. Then he said, with his hands on his hips, 'I'll answer your riddles if you take a swim in the river for an hour or two.'

"I shivered because that old river was full up with water and I hated water. So I thought, 'Well, maybe I just won't say anything and then he'll go away – he'll have to because he won't ever get the answers to my riddles, that's the truth.'

"But after two hours I was getting hungry and bored with Toki. I was just about to shake him off when he jumped up and said, 'There are ninety-three trillion, and seventy-five billion, and forty-three million and twenty-two stars in the whole heavens!'

"I said, 'How can you tell that?'

"He said if I didn't believe him then why didn't I count them. *Mmm!* I was f-u-m-i-n-g, but I let that one go. Next he says, 'See you, Dragon, you are the most brave creature in the whole upside-down world and the reason I know that is because you are hanging on by your jaggy tail looking at your reflection in the water. And everybody knows dragons are terrified of water, so to do what you're doing means you're very brave.'

"'You're so right,' I said, and I gave him that one too! But no way will he get the last one I was thinking to myself, so I said to him, 'Well, Toki my boy, not even the w-o-r-m-s in the bogli swamps know what I'm thinking right now and next to me they are the cleverest creatures, so there!'

"He didn't answer me and I could see he was getting nowhere, but begumps and begorgs, what did the little fella go and say at the last minute: 'You're thinking that I'm stupid and I'm going to walk away!'

"How could such a little runt know that? I got so angry with the cheeky chappy that I jumped up too far, toppled over the bridge and splashed into the killer water.

"But that brave lad, he swam in and pulled me out before all my scales fell off – he saved my life. Well, I had to let him go over the bridge then.

"After he came back from visiting his granny he told me he'd told her the story of what had happened to him and she'd had a good laugh, so much so it made her feel well again. He told me she said I should be a storyteller.

"I was brilliant at telling tales and, from that day to this, that's what I am – old Dragonory the tell-a-story monster."

Tattercoats

Retold by Pie Corbett

Once upon a time there was an old man who lived in a great house by the sea. He lived alone with his granddaughter, but he had sworn that he would never set eyes upon her again, for the day that she had been born was the day that his daughter had died.

He spent his days looking out at the sea till his hair grew white and his beard grew grey and his tears dripped on to the window sill where they wore a groove in the stone and flowed down to the sea.

Now the girl, she ran wild and grew up with no one to look after her. Sometimes she only had a few scraps from the kitchen and all she had to wear was an old petticoat. That was how she came to be called Tattercoats. And the servants, they knew their master did not care for her so they treated her cruelly with blows and harsh words.

Now the only time that she was
happy was when she ran free on the
heath with only the gooseherd for a
friend. He played his flute and she would
dance with the geese a-squabbling and
a-waddling along behind her.

Now one day news came that the
King was to hold a great ball, for it was
time for his only son, the Prince, to
choose a wife. When the invitation

arrived, the old man ordered his servants
to fetch a great pair of metal shears to cut
him loose, for his beard had grown so
long that it had wrapped round his legs
like chains and strapped him to his chair.
Then he sent for his white horse so that
he could ride to meet the King.

Poor Tattercoats, she sat by the
kitchen door crying because she could
not go to the ball. The nurse dared to ask

the old man not once, not twice but three times whether Tattercoats could travel with him, but he just rewarded her with scowls as dark as thunder.

So Tattercoats ran on to the heath for she wished to be alone. And while she was crying, her friend, the gooseherd, came by and said, "Let us travel to the town and we will see what we will see." So he played his flute and she danced down the road towards the town with the geese a-squabbling and a-waddling along behind her.

On the road, they met a handsome young man who stopped his horse and asked the way to the great ball. He dismounted and walked with Tattercoats. And as they walked, he looked at her and she looked at him – little sideways glances. Now the gooseherd played a few low notes like an owl calling at night – and the young man was so enchanted

with Tattercoats – that they fell deep, deep, deep. And a mile on down the lane, he asked her to marry him. But she just giggled, pushed him and said, "You'd be laughed to shame if you married a goosegirl. Go to the ball and find a fine lady but don't mock poor Tattercoats."

But the more she refused, the sweeter the flute played and the deeper they fell, till in the end he begged her to come to the ball at midnight, just as she was and he would dance with her, before them all, to prove his love.

So that night all the fine ladies and men were dancing but the Prince only had eyes for the clock. How slowly time crawled by! When midnight struck, Tattercoats, the gooseherd and all the geese flowed into the great hall. There was a silence as the fine ladies looked down their long noses and shuffled their jewels irritably.

How shocking!

How mocking!

Take that girl to the kitchen!

And the geese came a-squabbling and a-waddling along behind her.

But the Prince took her hand and danced the last dance while everyone watched. And when the dance was done, he spoke to the king, saying, "Father, this is the loveliest, liveliest girl in all the land and she is my choice."

And the gooseboy played a sweet tune with silvery notes that sparkled, and Tattercoats' rags shimmered into a shining, silver gown, gems glittering, with a golden crown on her head – and then the tune changed, growing faster and faster and the geese became dainty pages, dressed in sheer white. As Tattercoats and the Prince stepped up to the King, an old man with a roughly cut beard watched from the crowd with his

heart deadened by sorrow and his words
stopped like stones in his mouth, unable
to speak, unable to tell his granddaughter
how many mistakes it takes to carve tears
through stone.

So it was that Tattercoats married the
Prince who was brave enough to say
what he thought even though others
would mock and taunt and stare and
poke their fingers. And the King, he was
proud of his son and his one true love.

But the gooseherd was gone to play his flute elsewhere. And the old man, he rode back to his window by the sea where once he had sworn that he would never set eyes on his grandchild's face again.

So he is still there, waiting, waiting, till maybe one day just after this story ends, a young girl will come riding up to the house and run through the rooms with her shoes clacking on the floorboards and she will climb the stairs up to her grandfather's room, where maybe just after this story ends, she will open the door, dry his tears and cast new light into his life.

So run rabbit run, let this story be done.

Awongaleema

Retold by
Xanthe Gresham

Can you imagine a world without fruit, no juicy oranges or succulent strawberries? No apples to crunch or banana skins to slip on? Well, many years ago, way after the dinosaurs had died, but long before supermarkets were invented, there was a tree in the middle of the desert, and it was magic.

It was magic because it had a magical name. Because of this name, at its root there was a silver fountain that bubbled up and cascaded over. Because of this name, in the topmost branch of this tree, there was a golden bird that sang songs and told stories. But best of all this tree had growing on it every kind of fruit you could possibly think of. Papaya and mango, gooseberry and cranberry, pineapple and melon, kiwi fruit and cherry and all because of the tree's magical name.

One day, all the animals and the
human beings that gathered around the
tree forgot its name. I ask you, how
would you feel if your best friend came
up to you one day and went, "Hi, um,
ooh, what's your name?"

Well, the tree was so hurt that the
silver fountain dried up, the golden bird
flapped its wings and flew away and all
the fruit drooped, and sagged and fell.

Eeeee splat! Eeeee splat! Splat, splat, splat, splat, splat.

An old woman came forward, shaking her grey head and rubbing her dry hands. "We are so foolish, we have forgotten the name of the tree. And because of that, now we have no water, no songs and no food. And no one will be brave enough to go and see the mountain man. And yet he is the only one who can tell us how to get back the name of the tree, and where to find our sweet silver fountain and our beloved golden bird."

But all the animals put up their claws and wings and paws and snouts and squawked and squeaked and roared and howled, "Me, me, I'll go!"

The old woman had a difficult time choosing, but she finally decided to send the biggest, the heaviest, the strongest animal. "Elephant," she said, "Are you

really brave enough to go through rivers and deserts and forests and mountains to reach the mountain man and find out the name of the tree?"

Elephant trumpeted his reply, "Yes!" and off he went. Stamping through the forests, tramping up and down the mountains and wading through the rivers until he came to the mountain man, who was as tall as a hundred tower blocks stacked one on top of the other. He lifted up his trunk and boomed, "Mountain man, speak to me, tell me the name of the magic tree. Have you heard of the golden bird, or seen the silver fountain?"

The mountain man looked down from the clouds and replied in a voice that made the mountain behind him tremble.

"Yes, I've heard of the golden bird. I've seen the silver fountain. Awongaleema's the name of the tree, now you, Elephant, must climb the mountain. But don't look to the left, don't look to the right and don't look back or you will be turned to frozen stone."

Elephant began to climb the mountain. As he did so he looked to the left and to the right. He noticed that all around him were stones but they weren't

ordinary stones. They were stones that had once been animals. Monkeys, zebras, giraffes, lions, tigers, antelopes.

"Turn back," they whispered, "Turn back. You've forgotten the name of the magic tree."

And with a colossal stamp of frustration, Elephant looked back to ask the mountain man the name and, *bang!* he was turned to frozen stone.

Down below in the desert, the last leaf fell from the tree.

"Something has happened to Elephant," wailed the old woman, shaking her grey head. "Who else will be brave enough to travel?"

Once again, all of the animals volunteered to go. But this time, instead of the biggest she chose the fastest, fiercest animal. Cheetah went running through the deserts, leaping over mountains and swimming through rivers until he came to the mountain man. He roared towards the clouds, "Mountain man, speak to me, tell me the name of the magic tree. Have you heard of the golden bird or seen the silver fountain?"

The mountain man looked down from the clouds and replied in a voice that made the earth shake, "Yes, I've heard of the golden bird, I've seen the silver fountain. Awongaleema's the name of the tree, but you must climb the mountain. Don't look to the left, don't look to the right, and don't look back or you will be turned into frozen stone."

Cheetah bounded up the mountain but stopped. His ears twitching, his whiskers quivering as he looked left and right and noticed the frozen stones.

"Turn back, turn back. You've forgotten the name of the magic tree."

And with a flick of his tail, Cheetah turned and was frozen to stone. Down below in the desert, the bark of the tree began to crack. The animals whimpered and howled, and the old woman, her wrinkled face creasing more deeply than the bark of the dying tree said, "I'm going to send a small animal, a tiny animal – it's our last hope."

"*Meeeeek*," said the mouse, "I'll go, I'll go."

And so, she scurried and scampered

over the mountains and through the
forests. She wet her whiskers in the
rivers, and finally arrived at the mountain
man, ran up his bulging legs, perched on
his ear that was as big as a bush and
squeaked, "Mountain man, speak to me,
tell me the name of the magic tree. Have
you heard of the golden bird or seen the

silver fountain?"

The mountain man felt the tickling in the whiskers above his ear lobes. He raised his hand and picked up Mouse, holding her very close to his eyeball, which was as wide as the moon.

"Yes, I've heard of the golden bird. I've seen the silver fountain. Awongaleema's the name of the tree, but you must climb the mountain. Now, don't look to the left, don't look to the right and don't look back or you will be turned into frozen stone."

But Mouse was already wriggling out of his palm and running and repeating "Awongaleema, Awongaleema!" She didn't look left, she didn't look right. "Awongaleema, Awongaleema!"

The frozen stones echoed her cries, and from the top of the mountain came the sweetest notes of the golden bird. "Awongaleema." The bird sang and

fluttered over the silver fountain that
bubbled up and cascaded over. Mouse
was so overjoyed to see the golden bird,
so hot, so thirsty, so dry that she leapt
into the fountain, and splashed, diving
and shaking herself in the water. Little
drops of water touched the frozen stones,
and one by one they cracked open and

came to life. Monkeys, zebras, giraffes, lions, tigers, antelopes. They all returned to the dying tree in the dry desert, singing at the tops of their voices. "Awongaleema."

As Elephant, with Mouse on his head and Cheetah on his back, came into view, the animals around the tree went crazy with delight, wriggling, writhing, bucking, dancing, because as soon as it

heard its name, the tree burst into bud, flower and fruit. The silver fountain once more watered the tree and gave refreshment to the people and the animals. The golden bird settled on the topmost branch, and the people and the animals always had fruit, and they always had water and they always had songs and stories. And so may you.

The Snapdragon Plant

Retold by Taffy Thomas

It was an iron winter. The Dragon of Winter had curled itself around Moel Fammau, with its icy scales and tail sliding down into the Welsh Borders, Cheshire and beyond. The rivers Mersey and Dee were frozen solid; even part of the sea was frozen.

The ground was so hard that Mr Rose, the gardener, couldn't plant his plants or harvest his carrots or cabbage. Ships couldn't sail into the port of Liverpool with food from foreign parts. All the people who lived in that part of England fell on hard times.

So they went to the pompous Mayor and said, "You are going to have to do something about this." The Mayor said he would go and reason with the dragon and persuade him to go elsewhere.

He put on his climbing boots and warm clothes. Slipping and sliding, he climbed up Moel Fammau until he was staring into the icy blue eyes of the Dragon of Winter.

He said, "You are making my people very unhappy. They are not getting enough food and they are freezing. I am afraid you are going to have to go away."

And the dragon said, "But I love it here. I like the people here. I had no idea I was making them unhappy."

"I'm sorry," said the Mayor, "but you are going to have to go elsewhere."

And the dragon said, "Well, where might I go?"

"You could fly away to the frozen north and live on the ice cap with the polar bears and the Eskimos," replied the Mayor.

A tear came in to the dragon's icy blue eye. "But I like it here," he said.

"Well, I can see you are very unhappy," said the Mayor, "so we will have a compromise. What we will do is this: you can stay here for part of the year, and we will call that Winter; the time that you spend in the frozen north, we will call Summer; the time when you are flying north will be called Spring; and the time when you are coming back, we will call Autumn."

That was agreed and the Mayor returned down the mountain to the towns and villages. He told his people he had solved the problem. They were delighted, and said, "Well done, Mr Mayor," because they knew that Mr Mayor had been very brave to climb the mountain in that weather.

The next day the Dragon of Winter spread its white leathery wings and flew into the sky and headed for the north. The day after that, the sun came out bright and strong. Mr Rose, the gardener, could get back to work in his garden, the fishermen could go out and fish in the Dee and the Mersey, and ships from afar could again bring food into the docks in Liverpool and Birkenhead.

All the people had smiles on their faces and all was well. When autumn came it started to get cold again, and again the Dragon of Winter returned to its favourite place and curled itself around the peak of Moel Fammau. All the people were cold, but they thought, "That's all right, because he'll fly away before too long."

But when it came time for winter to end, the dragon was still there. Again the people went to the Mayor, and the

Mayor said, "That dragon is very, very naughty. It has not kept to our agreement. The dragon is bad."

A little boy in the crowd stood up and said, "No, the dragon is not bad, because I really like throwing snowballs and sledging in the snow. And I like wearing warm jumpers and hearing stories by the fireside in winter."

But all the people said, "Look, we are starving again. Something has got to be done."

And the little boy said, "I'll go up and have a word with the dragon."

"Could you – a small child – do better with the dragon than me?" said the Mayor.

"Please let me try," said the little boy. He put on his best boots and his warmest clothes and climbed the mountain until he was staring into the dragon's icy blue eyes.

He said, "You're not supposed to be here now. You should have flown to the frozen north and the sun should be out. Although I really like playing in the snow and the ice when you are here, I also enjoy mucking about in the garden with my Uncle Joe in the summer."

The dragon said, "Look, I am ever so sorry if I have upset you again, but I am a little confused. You see, I don't know when I am supposed to go."

"Let me help you," said the boy. "When I am in the garden with my Uncle Joe, we plant a plant that shows us when it is the spring and summer. We call that flower a snapdragon because, if you look at it, it has a face like yours. And if I squeeze it and its mouth opens, I can make it talk just like you. So if you keep your eye on the garden, when you see that plant growing you will know that is time to head to the frozen north; that is your sign."

The dragon thanked him, smiled, stretched its white leathery wings, and again headed for the polar ice cap and the white bears of the frozen north.

And the little boy put on his thinner clothes and went out in the garden to play with Uncle Joe and plant those plants that we call snapdragons.

The Snapdragon Plant

The Papaya that Spoke

Retold by Pie Corbett

Once upon a time there was farmer who lived in a village. One day he felt hungry so he went out to pick a papaya. To his amazement, the papaya spoke. "Hands off!"

The farmer looked at his dog. "Did you say that?" said the farmer.

"No," said the dog. "It was the papaya!"

"*Aaaaargh!*" screamed the farmer. As fast as his legs could carry him, he ran

and he ran and he ran till he came to a market, where he met a fisherman selling fish.

"Why are you running so fast when the sun is shining so bright?" asked the fisherman.

"First a papaya spoke to me and next my dog!" replied the farmer.

"That's impossible," said the fisherman.

"Oh, no it isn't," said one of the fish. "*Aaaaargh!*" screamed the farmer. As fast as his legs could carry him, he ran and he ran and he ran till he came to a field, where he met a shepherd with his goats.

"Why are you running so fast when the sun is shining so bright?" asked the shepherd.

"First a papaya spoke to me, next my dog and after that a fish!" replied the farmer.

"That's impossible," said the shepherd.

"Oh, no it isn't," bleated one of the goats.

"*Aaaaargh!*" screamed the farmer. As fast as his legs could carry him, he ran and he ran and he ran till he came to the village, where he met the King sitting on his wooden rocking chair.

"Why are you running so fast when the sun is shining so bright?" asked the King.

"First a papaya spoke to me, next my dog, after that a fish and finally a goat!"

"That's impossible," said the King. "Get out of here, you foolish man." So the poor farmer walked home with his head hung down.

The King rocked back and forth, back and forth, back and forth. "How silly of him to imagine that things can talk."

There was a long silence – and then the chair spoke! "Quite so – whoever heard of a talking papaya?"

The Papaya that Spoke

The Liar

Retold by Helen Frances

There was once a King who was *bored* of being King.

He was bored of being on best behaviour at big banquets.

He was bored of opening brand-new buildings by snipping ribbons and making small speeches.

He was bored of sailing out in his royal yacht and waving to his subjects on the shore.

He was bored of listening to his ministers making up nasty new rules in meetings.

And he was very, very, very, very, very bored of having to wear his crown all the time.

"Just for *once* in my life," he said, "I'd like to…

"Play with my food! I'd make jelly babies cry, squash butternut pie, and magic Welsh rarebit out of hats!

"Just for *twice* in my life," he said, "I'd like to…

"Bash down a building with a very big crane with a ball and chain.

"Just for *thrice* in my life," he said, "I'd like to…

"Sail the seven seas in my royal yacht and visit new places.

"Just for *fourth* in my life," he said, "I'd like to…

"Shout *hooray!* at the end of ministerial meetings, slide down the banisters, stamp in big puddles and bark back at noisy dogs.

"But most of all, for *fifth*, I'd like to…

"Swap hats! I'd like to trifle with a trilby, piffle with a panama, boffle with a boater, gliffle with a deerstalker, spoffle with a baseball cap! I'd like to go to the dogs in an old flat cap. I'd like to be comfortable for a change.

"But I can't!" said the King.

"It's not fair!" said the King.

"Don't despair!" said the Prince and Princess, and they whispered in the King's ear.

The King smiled…

The next day the King issued a royal challenge, in his best handwriting, on a royal scroll.

The King's heralds read out the King's royal challenge to everyone in the town.

"Whosoever can tell the King the biggest, funniest, longest, wittiest, coolest, wickedest, pottiest, zaniest LIE will receive a prize of ONE SOLID-GOLD APPLE."

Next day, a gypsy arrived at the palace. Her clothes were torn and her feet were bare, but she told the story of Bold Mary and the Fox. It was the most wonderful story the King had ever heard! He didn't think it was true, but he

didn't want to argue with her, so he
didn't give the golden apple to the gypsy.

Next day, a tinker arrived at the
palace. His clothes were torn and his
boots were holey, but he told the story of
The Most Precious Object. It was the
most wonderful story the King had ever
heard! He didn't think it was true, but he

wanted to hear it again, so he didn't give the golden apple to the tinker.

Next day, a lady arrived at the palace. She wore silken skirts and her slippers were embroidered with gold, but she told the story of Sinbad the Sailor. It was the most wonderful story the King had ever heard! He didn't think it was true, but he wanted the adventures of Sinbad to go on for ever, so he didn't give the golden apple to the lady.

Next day, a clown arrived at the palace. He wore silly-billy clothes and red-and-yellow shoes, but he told the story of the Ship of Fools. It was the most wonderful story the King had ever heard! He didn't think it was true, but he wanted it to be true, so he didn't give the golden apple to the clown.

Next day, a musician arrived at the palace. She wore rings on her fingers and played violin, and she told the story of

the Cow's Shoulder Blade. It was the most wonderful story the King had ever heard! He didn't think it was true, but he wanted to hear more and more and more stories, so he didn't give the golden apple to the musician.

The King had never felt better in his life! He forgot all about being on best behaviour and snipping ribbons, waving politely to his subjects and sitting for ages in ministerial meetings… best of all, he even forgot there was a crown on his head!

One day, an old woman came to the palace. She carried a large empty jar in her arms.

"Well?" said the King, "How can I help you?"

"It's this," said old woman. "You remember, surely? You owe me this jar full of gold. I've come to collect it."

"You perfect liar!" shouted the King. "I owe you no gold!"

"A liar, am I?" said old woman, "Then give me the golden apple!"

The King began to fidget. The King began to sweat. The King said, "Um, perhaps you aren't a liar after all…"

"Well, if I'm not a liar, give me the pot of gold you owe me!" said old woman. So the King handed over the golden apple. Old woman was very happy with the golden apple. It was beautiful.

And after that the King was very happy, because he thought up a nice new rule, all for himself. On Thursdays, it was his day off.

On Thursdays, the King… slides down the banisters, draws faces on his breakfast toast, shouts *'hooray!'* and turns cartwheels because he's cancelled all his meetings. Then he runs away with the Prince and Princess to bash down buildings with a big ball and crane. After that, they sail the seven seas, they discover new kinds of hat to wear, and they all come back at night for a special surprise tea.

And the King invites… the gypsy, the tinker, the lady, the clown, the musician, old woman and old woman's grandchildren back to the palace every Thursday evening! They tell each other stories, play music and tell jokes and riddles. And plenty of other people are there too...

The Old Man and the Donkey

Retold by Pie Corbett

An old man and his grandson were taking their donkey to market to sell. The donkey walked ahead of them and they both walked behind, talking little bits of this and little bits of that.

So on they went, jiggety-jog, jiggety-jog, jiggety-jog.

Sooner rather than later, an onlooker said, "What's this? You've got a donkey and yet you make this poor little boy walk in the heat of the day?"

Thoughtfully, the old man put the little boy on to the donkey's back and off they set. The boy enjoyed resting his legs.

So on they went, jiggety-jog, jiggety-jog, jiggety-jog.

Sooner rather than later, another onlooker said, "What's this? You lazy little boy, making your old grandpa walk while you ride at your ease!"

Embarrassed, the little boy clambered down and the old man struggled on to the donkey's back himself. The old man enjoyed resting his weary limbs.

So on they went, jiggety-jog, jiggety-jog, jiggety-jog.

Sooner rather than later, another onlooker said, "What is this? You let such a young boy run along beside you, while you rest on your donkey's back!"

Gratefully, the boy climbed on to the donkey's back as well.

So on they went, jiggety-jog, jiggety-jog, jiggety-jog.

Sooner rather than later, a final onlooker said, "What's this? You let a poor old donkey carry both of you. Surely, it cannot be your donkey. You are treating it so cruelly!" So that poor old man no longer knew what to do for the best.

Confused, he bound the donkey's legs together with some cord. In that way, they tried to carry the donkey hanging from a pole between them all the way to the market.

Everyone laughed at such a ridiculous sight! It upset the old man so much that he set the donkey loose in the fields and went back home with his grandson, empty-handed.

And the moral of the story is that if you try to please everyone, you will end up pleasing no one – not even yourself.

The Old Man and the Donkey

Mulenga and the Cherries

Retold by Pie Corbett

One day, Mulenga went shopping with his mother. Their first call was to the greengrocer's. While his mother was buying some fruits, Mulenga looked longingly at a box containing juicy red cherries.

"Help yourself to a handful, Mulenga," said the greengrocer, but Mulenga did not move.

"I'm sure you like cherries, don't you?" asked the puzzled shopkeeper. Mulenga nodded his head quickly.

Thinking that the boy was too shy to help himself, the greengrocer went to the box and gave Mulenga a large handful.

When they left the shop, Mulenga's mother asked him why he'd not taken the cherries when the greengrocer had told him to.

"Well you see, mummy," answered Mulenga, "his hand is twice as big as mine!"

Spider's Wife

Retold by Helen East

Astory, a story here it comes, there it lands. Where does it land? On Spider's head.

Oh-ho Spider! What a fine fellow! Good looking, good talker, good drummer too! Everybody's dancing when he comes around. Everyone's happy – except perhaps Spider's wife. Maybe she sees things the others don't see.

One day there was a big famine. Spider kept drumming, making people forget their troubles, so they gave him something here and there – a bite of food, a bit of money, a bowl of palm wine.

But Spider was only caring for himself. Whatever he got, and it wasn't a lot, it was all gone by the time he came home. His wife and children got nothing except thinner and thinner every day.

Ai! Ai! His wife complained to her friends, but what could they do?

"Men are men. They do as they like," they said. "That's how life is – there's no good fighting against it."

Eh! Eh! His wife complained to Spider himself. But he was a husband like any other. He couldn't let his wife tell him what to do!

Ah well, as they say, "No good comes from struggling against the stream."

Oh yes! Everyone agrees – except perhaps Spider's wife. Maybe she sees things the others don't see.

Spider. *Mmm!* One morning he was passing Cow's house, when he saw a big bucket of milk put aside in the shade. No one was looking … it smelt good. Spider licked his lips, and climbed up to have a sip.

But, oh! The side was slithery, and suddenly he slid – *splash!* – right into the middle of all that milk. Well, at first he was happy, swimming round and drinking. But when he tried to get out, he found he was stuck, and then he started crying and shouting.

Spider's wife heard, and came running to help. But when she tried to pull him out, she slipped herself, and – *splosh!* – there she was in the milk as well.

They tried and they tried and they tried to climb out, but it was no good. And now Spider was quite tired out.

"*Ai! Ai! Ai!* We are both going to drown," he sighed. "Might as well give up now. No good struggling against the stream."

But Spider's wife, she didn't agree. Maybe she saw things he didn't see.

"Hold on to me!" she said, and for once her husband did as he was told.

Round and round and round she swam, kicking her legs and struggling on. And little by little, with all that splashing and thrashing, the milk began to get thicker ... and thicker ... until at last it started turning to butter. Then when it was solid enough, they both clambered out.

So they went home covered in butter, and all the children feasted on it.

And Spider's wife was happy to see them fed.

"It's good that I did struggle on," she said.

And Spider? Well that lesson landed right on his head. And you've heard it too. So maybe it landed on you.

Little Leo and the Moon Rabbit

Retold by
Jackie Andrews

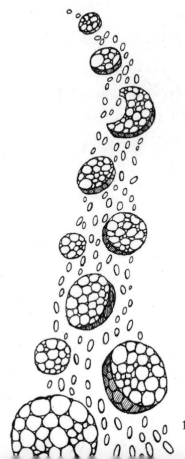

Little Leo lived in a monastery in the snowy mountains of Tibet. He was a sentinel dog; he kept watch for the monks and warned them whenever a stranger was coming. Every day he sat in his special window in the wall beside the gate, watching the mountain path.

As soon as he saw a traveller coming, Little Leo would bark and run and tell the monks.

It was a very long, hard climb up to the monastery, so it gave the monks plenty of time to get ready for their visitor. As soon as they arrived, Little Leo would jump down and welcome them at the gate.

One evening, Little Leo was sitting peacefully in his window seat when he saw the Moon Rabbit jump off the moon. Down and down the Moon Rabbit floated … right to the foot of the mountain, his large ears spreading out like a parachute to break his fall. Then the Moon Rabbit picked himself up, dusted himself down, and set off up the path to the monastery.

Little Leo was a bit scared and a little bit excited to see the Moon Rabbit coming up the track. He ran to tell his friends.

"The Moon Rabbit is coming!" he told his friend, Yak.

"Oh dear, Little Leo," said Yak, shaking his shaggy head. "You don't want to have anything to do with the Moon Rabbit. Tricky, he is. He'll try and take you back to the moon with him. You must be very careful."

"Why would he want to take me back to the moon?" asked Little Leo. But Yak wouldn't say any more, so Little Leo went to find Painted Dragon.

"The Moon Rabbit is coming!"

Little Leo told Painted Dragon.

"Oh dear, Little Leo," said Painted Dragon. "You don't want to have anything to do with the Moon Rabbit. Secretive, he is. See how the moonlight hides all my nice colours? It's just the same with Moon Rabbit: he keeps things hidden!"

"What does he need to hide?" asked Little Leo. But Painted Dragon wouldn't say any more, so Little Leo went to see Brother Lhakpa.

"Brother Lhakpa, the Moon Rabbit is coming," said Little Leo. "What should I do? I don't want him to trick me and take me to the moon with him."

"Don't worry so, Little Leo," said Brother Lhakpa. "Remember, we never turn anyone away, especially anyone who needs our help. Welcome the Moon Rabbit and see what he wants. Then listen to what your heart tells you."

Little Leo went back to his window in the wall just as the Moon Rabbit climbed the last few steps up the path.

"Welcome, Brother Rabbit," said Little Leo, with only a little shake in his voice. "What brings you to our monastery?"

"Good evening, Little Leo," replied the Moon Rabbit. "You'll never believe it, but I was hanging out my socks to dry when a great gust of wind blew me right off the moon and down to your mountain. I've come to ask for your help to get home."

Little Leo looked carefully at the Moon Rabbit. Then he looked up at the moon. It looked a very long way away.

"Come in and rest," said Little Leo, "and we'll think about what to do."

Little Leo took the Moon Rabbit to one of the guest rooms and served him green tea and rice cakes. And while he ate, the Moon Rabbit entertained Little Leo, between mouthfuls, with many wonderful stories. Finally, he curled up in a blanket and went to sleep.

For the rest of that night, Little Leo looked out of his window, thinking about how to get the Moon Rabbit back to the moon, and listening to his heart. Then, just as the sun was rising, he noticed a dragonfly skimming over the monastery garden. It gave him an idea.

While the Moon Rabbit slept on, Little Leo worked hard on his idea. It involved a lot of wooden sticks, paper and string. At last, it was ready. Little Leo had made a beautiful dragonfly kite.

He waited until sunset, then he went to wake the Moon Rabbit.

Little Leo took the Moon Rabbit out on to the mountainside. There was a strong breeze blowing and everywhere was bathed in silvery moonlight. Little Leo showed the Moon Rabbit his kite and explained how it would take him back to the moon. He also held out a bag of rice balls for Moon Rabbit to take with him on his journey.

The Moon Rabbit looked up at the moon, then he looked at Little Leo and his kite. A sneaky look appeared in his eyes.

"It's a beautiful kite…" he began, and his voice became drowsy and magical… "Have you ever been to the moon?" the Moon Rabbit asked, as he helped himself to a rice ball. "It's peaceful and quiet. Just the sort of place you'd like… *mmphf!*"

Suddenly the Moon Rabbit couldn't speak any more. The rice ball had very sticky toffee hidden inside it, and had quite glued his teeth together. Little Leo shook his head – for the Moon Rabbit's voice had started to make him feel very sleepy.

Quickly, before the Moon Rabbit realised what was happening, Little Leo tied him up with the string of the dragonfly kite.

"Little Leo, what have you done?" asked the Moon Rabbit as soon as he was able.

"I knew you would try to persuade me to go back to the moon with you,"

Little Leo explained. "But I watched you jump from the moon – the wind didn't blow you here, and you don't wear socks. And though you told me wonderful stories, you didn't once tell me anything about yourself…" Little Leo paused. "Or how lonely you are."

The Moon Rabbit hung his head. A

large tear fell down from his cheek.

"I don't have any friends on the moon," he said at last.

"Brother Lhakpa says that friendship must be a free gift," said Little Leo. "Otherwise it will wither and die like a flower picked from a plant. If you took me away from my friends, I would be very unhappy too. But we can still be friends. You can come and visit us any time."

"You're very wise, Little Leo," said the Moon Rabbit. "I'm sorry I tried to trick you. Let us be friends! Now, help me off this mountain and I will go home."

Little Leo gave a sharp bark. Yak quickly came up behind the Moon Rabbit and with a quick biff from his great head, launched him into space.

They watched and waved as the dragonfly kite carrying the Moon

Rabbit sailed into the wind, up and up, all the way to the moon. Then Yak lumbered back to his stall and Little Leo went to find Brother Lhakpa. Brother Lhakpa was waiting with a bowl of green tea and Little Leo's favourite rice cakes.

"You did very well today, Little Leo," he said, his eyes twinkling. "You listened to your heart and your head! Perhaps one day you might give me the recipe for those special rice balls — I can think of quite a few talkative people I'd like to share them with!" He chuckled at the thought.

Little Leo felt very happy. He curled himself up by Brother Lhakpa's feet, underneath his blanket. And just before he fell asleep, Little Leo was sure he saw his new friend, the Moon Rabbit, waving to him from the moon.

Bimwili and the Zimwi

Retold by Jane Grell

Long ago in a village in Zanzibar lived three sisters with their mother and father. They were Tete, Tasha and the youngest, Bimwili. During the school holidays the two older girls loved going to the sea for a swim. Bimwili was never allowed to go as she was still little. One day, however, Bimwili begged her sisters to take her along.

"No, Bimwili," they said. "You are much too little and the road to the sea is long and full of danger. "

Bimwili pleaded with her mother to let her go but her big sisters would not hear of it.

"You will only get in the way," they said.

Bimwili's mother must have felt sorry for her. "Tete and Tasha," she said firmly, "if you don't take your little sister with you, you can't go either."

So that is how Bimwili got to tag along behind her sisters.

The way to the sea was long but the colourful fruit trees, birds, monkeys and other animals were enchanting. When they got to the beach, Tete and Tasha quickly removed their sarongs and dived into the waves. As she was not yet able to swim, Bimwili happily played at the water's edge.

As she paddled, one of the waves rolled towards her carrying something pink which landed at her feet.

"A shell, a shell!" she cried with joy. Bimwili sat on a rock to examine her

shell. She ran her fingers over the spiky surface. She liked the feel of the smooth, pink inside which made a whispering sound when she held it to her ear. She even made up a song about it:

> "*I have a shell from out of the sea,*
> *A shell the big wave gave to me.*
> *It's pink inside like the sunset sky,*
> *And in it you hear the ocean sigh.*"

Bimwili left the shell on the rock and went back to playing with the waves.

After a few hours Tete and Tasha decided it was time to go home. Halfway home Bimwili suddenly stopped and cried, "My shell! I forgot my shell. Come with me, Tete and Tasha."

But her sisters were very cross. Tete complained, "Bimwili, I knew you would be a bother."

Tasha said, "We will find your shell the next time we come back to the sea, Bimwili."

But Bimwili was determined, so she went back on her own. To stop herself being afraid, she sang her shell song. When she got to the sea, sitting on the rock where she had left her shell was a horrible Zimwi. His arms were long and dangly and his face was like an old, shrivelled watermelon.

"Jambo, my little singer," he said. "How beautifully you sing."

"Jambo," replied Bimwili. "Please can I have my shell back?"

"Come closer. That's right. Closer," said the Zimwi. "Sing to me again and you can have your shell."

Bimwili sang in a frightened little voice, "*I have a shell from out of the sea.*"

"No, no, no. Louder. Sing louder and come closer," said the Zimwi.

When Bimwili got really close, he grabbed her and put her in his big drum along with the shell and closed it up.

"I've got you, my little singer," the Zimwi grinned. "Now I shall be famous because I have the world's only singing drum. When I beat the drum, you – my little singer – must sing your song."

The Zimwi picked up his drum and set off down a path. He came to a village. "Gather round, gather round," he called. "I have a drum that can sing. Cook me a meal and I shall entertain you."

The Zimwi tapped on his drum and a little voice sang. The villagers were delighted and they let the Zimwi eat and drink as much as he liked. Then on to the next village.

Meanwhile, Tete and Tasha arrived home without their little sister.

"Where is Bimwili?" asked their mother. "How you could you have left her to walk the path alone? Go back at once."

But when they got to the sea there was no sign of Bimwili. Tete and Tasha went home feeling very sad. Their father sent out a search party with torches to look for Bimwili. They searched in vain for days.

During all this time, Bimwili lived squashed up in the Zimwi's drum with her shell. She ate wild berries, coconuts and bananas from the forest. All she had to do was sing the same song over and over. Sometimes she changed the words and the Zimwi didn't even notice.

One day, they arrived at another village.

"Gather round, gather round," shouted the Zimwi, in his usual way. "I have the world's only singing drum," he boasted. "My drum doesn't go gum, gum, gum. My drum can sing a beautiful song. Bring me food and drink and I will entertain you."

A voice asked, "Bwana Zimwi, what would you like with your rice, chicken or fish?"

Bimwili's heart leapt. That was her mother's voice. This was her village. When the Zimwi beat the drum she sang:

"I have a shell from out of the sea;
A shell the Zimwi stole from me.
It's dark in here like the midnight sky;
If you listen you'll hear Bimwili sigh!"

As she was rather busy, Bimwili's mother did not hear the song of the drum but her sisters Tete and Tasha did.

"Mother! Mother!" they whispered. "That's Bimwili in the drum."

So when the Zimwi was about to eat, Bimwili's mother gave him a pitcher and said:

"Bwana Zimwi, could you please fetch some water from the river?"

While the Zimwi was gone, Bimwili's father opened the drum and lifted out a smiling Bimwili. He then filled the drum with sand and put the top back on.

After the Zimwi had eaten, someone said to him, "Now, give us another song on your drum before you go."

The Zimwi began to beat the drum but no song came.

"Sing, drum, sing!" he scolded, but the drum would not sing. The people laughed their heads off. Angrily the Zimwi picked up his drum and left in rather a hurry.

That night, when the grown-ups sat under the banyan tree, telling their

favourite tales by moonlight, Bimwili
too had a story to tell and a song to sing.
What's more, they passed her shell round
so all could hear the soothing *ssh, ssh* of
the sea.

Matiwara's Name Game

Retold by Usha Bahl

At the edge of the savannah there were lots of acacia trees. In the middle of the acacia trees, stood a small house with a thorny fence. A mysterious old woman lived in the house. Nobody knew anything about her. Nobody visited her, but there were lots of stories about her in all the nearby villages.

There was a little girl called Matiwara living with the old woman. Where did she come from? Who was she? Nobody knew anything about her. One of the stories talked about a spell cast on Matiwara by the old woman so that Matiwara could never leave her.

Matiwara did all the housework for the old woman. She cleaned the house, dusted the house, gathered firewood and cooked for the old woman.

The old woman was always angry and never happy with Matiwara. This made Matiwara very miserable.

"Please tell me how I can set myself free and live in a village like all the other people," Matiwara asked the old woman.

"Haa haa haa! Hee hee hee!
You can never set yourself free,"

sang the old woman as she curled up by the fire to go to sleep.

This went on for a few days and a few nights.

One night Matiwara cooked the old woman's favourite dinner, which was fried corn with grated coconut, yellow guavas and ripe mangoes. It was delicious and the old woman was really happy after eating it.

Matiwara took this opportunity to ask her again. "Please, dear lady, tell me the secret to set myself free."

"Haa haa haa! Hee hee hee!
You'll never guess that to be free
You must find the name given to me,"

sang the old lady.

Matiwara jumped for joy. She set to work guessing and collecting names from that very evening. Every day Matiwara sat by the fire after a long day's hard work and tried to guess the old woman's name.

"Is your name Rampala, Jumbona, Sabina, Deggee, Mambo or Sabulana?" asked Matiwara.

"No, no, no," replied the old woman.

"Is your name…?"

"You can try, try, try, but you cannot find my name. It is a big secret. Only I know my name and I'll never tell it to anyone ever, ever in my life."

Matiwara was very disappointed. She could not eat or sleep. She could not finish her day's work. The old woman was always angry with her.

One day Matiwara forgot to collect the firewood so she had to rush into the woods to collect it before dark. She soon lost her way and went deeper and deeper into the woods. It was beginning to get dark. Matiwara had to hurry up and find her way back. When suddenly she came across a clearing in the woods. She hid

behind an acacia tree. She could see a fire burning in the middle of the clearing. There was nobody about.

She stood very still and listened. She

could hear the night calls of the animals. Suddenly … a loud cackle shook the silence. The old woman appeared from behind the trees carrying some acacia thorns. She threw them on to the fire and the flames leapt up high.

The old woman then began to dance round the fire singing,

"Haa haa haa! Hee hee hee!
She'll never guess it, she'll never be free.
She must find the name given to me.
Haa haa haa! Hee hee hee!
It's Shokolokobangoshey.
It's Shokolokobangoshey."

Matiwara heard the name clearly. She almost shouted out for joy, but she slowly crept away and made her way back to the house.

The old woman arrived, looking very tired, and asked Matiwara, "Have you got my soup ready?"

"No. I have been busy finding new names for you today," replied Matiwara.

"Oh. Oh. You have been naughty. I am going to punish you. Where is my stick?" and the old lady started to look for her stick.

"Is your name Aaa Zoom Big-a-Zum?" asked Matiwara.

"No, no," replied the old woman. "And I am tired and hungry. Give me my dinner quickly."

"Just one more then," pleaded Matiwara. "Is your name – eh – Shoko, Shokoloko – Shokolokobangoshey?" Lightning flashed across the sky and lit up the acacia trees…

"No, no, yes," said the old woman as she stood still. "I am Shokolokobangoshey."

Lightning flashed again. Matiwara closed her eyes and found herself in her own village with her own family. She had forgotten everything about the old woman.

A strong wind blew and the old woman disappeared in the tall sandy grass of the savannah.

Nobody has ever seen her again. But the villagers say that if you stand on the edge of the savannah, you can hear, "Shokolokobangoshey, Shokolokobangoshey," as the wind blows through the tall sandy savannah grass.

The Monster Over the Hill

Retold by Daniel Morden

There was once a town near a mountain. On the other side of the mountain there was a monster.

Each day clouds of bitter smoke from the monster's nostrils billowed over the mountain and killed the crops. A yellow dust settled over everything. The river was cloudy with a yellow silt.

At night, no one slept because the monster's roars shook their houses. The cows would not give milk. The chickens would not lay eggs.

Eventually the Mayor called a meeting. The people gathered before him, handkerchiefs over their faces to protect them from the smoke.

The Mayor shouted, "We can't live our lives this way! For the sake of our children, something must be done! If all of us went together, climbed the mountain and confronted the beast, I know we could overcome it!"

Silence. The Mayor could not find a single pair of eyes to meet his own. "Constable?"

"I would help you," said the constable, "but I have a family. If I don't return, who will provide for them? Let those without children go."

"Blacksmith?"

"I want to go with you, but people need me! Without me shoeing their horses they can't plough their fields! I make the blades of their tools! I have a responsibility to them. Let others go."

"Farmer?"

"I would go with you, but I must care for my beasts. That is why God put me here, not so that I could fight a monster. Let others go."

One by one they made their excuses, until the Mayor said, "I would go by myself, but you have voted me your

Mayor. I would be betraying my duty to you if I walked away knowing I would never return."

And then a little girl said, "I'll go!"

"What?" said the Mayor. "You? But you're only a child."

"Someone has to go. The constable's family have terrible dreams if they can sleep at all. The horses the blacksmith shoes hide in the back of their stables.

They have to be dragged out to plough the fields. The farmer's beasts won't eat their food. I will go and fight this creature."

"You mustn't. What is the point in you throwing away your life? You are just one child. You can do nothing," her mother and father pleaded with her.

The girl was silent. That night, as the walls of her bedroom shook, she thought and thought. Should she go?

Next morning, before her parents had risen, she dressed herself and crept from her bedroom. She set off through the village, between the houses where the people cowered in their beds.

Up the yellow mountain she went. Every step took a little more effort. She was shaking from head to foot.

She got to the top – and she saw it. It was huge and horrible. It roared at her. She swallowed hard and walked towards it, shouting back.

As she walked, a strange thing happened. The closer she got, the smaller it became.

Now it was the size of a house.

Now the size of an elephant.

Now the size of a cow.

Now the size of a dog.

Now the size of a cat.

Now the size of a mouse.

She knelt and picked it up. It tried to roar. Out came a squeak.

She said, "What is your name?"

"My name is Fear."

Lazy Jack

Retold by Pie Corbett

Once upon a time there was a lazy boy called Jack, who lived with his mother. Unfortunately, they were very poor. His mother worked hard spinning. However, Jack did nothing. In the summer, he basked in the sun. In the winter, he dozed by the fire.

One day his mother said that if he didn't work for his porridge, she would throw him out of the house.

So Jack went to work for a farmer. At the end of the day he was paid one bright new penny, but on the way home he dropped it in a stream.

"You stupid boy," said his mother. "You should have put it in your pocket."

"I'll do so next time," promised Jack.

The next day, Jack went to work for the farmer again. At the end of the day, he was paid with a jar of milk.

Remembering what his mother had

told him, Jack tipped it into his pocket.

"You stupid boy," said his mother. "You should have carried it on your head."

"I'll do so next time," promised Jack. The next day, Jack went to work for a miller. At the end of the day, he was paid with a tomcat for catching mice. Remembering what his mother had told him, Jack tied it on to his head.

"You stupid boy," said his mother. "You should have tied it up with string, to lead it along behind you."

"I'll do so next time," promised Jack.

The next day, Jack went to work for a baker. At the end of the day he was paid with a roast chicken. Remembering what his mother had told him, he tied it up with string and pulled it along behind him.

"You ninny hammer," said his mother. "You should have put it in your knapsack."

"I'll do so next time," promised Jack.

The next day, Jack went to work for a cattle-keeper. At the end of the day, he was paid with a donkey. Remembering what his mother had told him, he tried to squeeze it into his knapsack.

On his way home, Jack passed the house of a beautiful girl. Long ago, the doctors had said that she would not speak or find happiness until she had laughed.

As a result, her wealthy father had said that the person who could make her laugh would surely make her happy for the rest of her life.

Along came Jack with the donkey on his back and its legs poking into the air. Now the sight was so strange and so comical that the girl burst out laughing!

So it happened that Jack became both happy and wealthy, despite his foolish ways.

Snip snap snout,
My story is out!

Master of
all Masters

Retold by
Joseph Jacobs

Agirl once went to the fair to hire herself for servant. At last a funny-looking old gentleman engaged her and took her home to his house. When she got there he told her that he had something to teach her, for that in his house he had his own names for things.

He said to her, "What will you call me?"

"Master or mister, or whatever you please, sir," says she.

"You must call me master of all masters. And what would you call this?" he said, pointing to his bed.

"Bed or couch, or whatever you please, sir."

"No, that's my barnacle. And what do you call these?" said he, pointing to his pantaloons.

"Breeches or trousers, or whatever you please, sir."

"You must call them squibs and crackers. And what would you call her?" pointing to the cat.

"Cat or kit, or whatever you please, sir."

"You must call her white-faced simminy. And this now," showing the fire, "what would you call this?"

"Fire or flame, or whatever you please, sir."

"You must call it hot cockalorum. And what this?" he went on, pointing to the water.

"Water or wet, or whatever you please, sir."

"No, pondalorum is its name. And what do you call all this?" asked he, as he pointed to the house.

"House or cottage, or whatever you please, sir."

"You must call it high topper mountain."

That very night the servant woke her master up in a fright and said, "Master of all masters, get out of your barnacle and put on your squibs and crackers. For white-faced simminy has got a spark of hot cockalorum on its tail, and unless you get some pondalorum, high topper mountain will be all on hot cockalorum."

That's all.

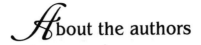

About the authors

Xanthe Gresham

Xanthe Gresham (pronounced "Zanthee") is a full-time storyteller. She began storytelling in 1995 and is popular with both adults and children. She has worked in the UK, Ireland, France, New Zealand, Slovenia, Holland and Switzerland.

She has worked extensively for The British Museum. She works as a storyteller for Holland Park and The Chelsea Physic Garden and is a Lecturer in Storytelling and Drama at the University of East London.

Taffy Thomas

Taffy Thomas is a leading and experienced storyteller. He has a repertoire of more than 300 stories, collected mainly from oral sources.

He has appeared at arts festivals in the USA and in Norway. In 2001 he performed for the Blue Peter Prom at the Royal Albert Hall; and in 2006 was storyteller in residence at the National Centre for Storytelling in Tennessee. Taffy is currently the artistic director of Tales in Trust, the Northern Centre for Storytelling, in the Lake District. In the 2001, he was awarded an MBE for services to storytelling and charity. He tours nationally and internationally working both in entertainment and education and is also a patron of the Society for Storytelling.

Pie Corbett

Pie Corbett is an extremely well known and prominent figure in the field of education. He has worked as a primary teacher and headteacher and has also worked as an English inspector in Gloucestershire.

Pie edits, compiles and writes poetry books for children. He also writes resource books for teachers. He has published over 200 books and is a selector for the 'Children's Poetry Bookshelf'. He also wrote poetry objectives for the National Literacy Strategy. In addition, he has also appeared at numerous literary festivals such as those at Cheltenham, Edinburgh and Wiltshire.

Jackie Andrews

Children's writer and editor Jackie Andrews, first worked as a library assistant and then as a teacher of English, Art and Drama. Her first novel for teenagers *Blood Feud,* was published in 2004, followed by *Deadly Encounters* in 2006. Now retired, Jackie lives in Warwickshire with fifteen rabbits, ten guinea pigs, two bantam hens and two Lhasa Apso dogs – but still tries to find time to write.

Jane Grell

Jane Grell was born on the island of Dominica. She has been running storytelling workshops for children and adults since 1986. Now living in London, she has taken her stories to audiences around the UK. She draws heavily though not exclusively on her African-Caribbean heritage. Her storytelling thus consists of rhythm games, songs, poems, proverbs, riddles and stories. Jane's stories have been published in various anthologies.

Daniel Morden
Daniel Morden is one of the UK's most popular storytellers. He regularly appears at The National Theatre and The Barbican Centre. His recent book, *Dark Tales from the Woods*, won the Welsh Books Council Tir Na Nog prize.

Andrew Fusek Peters
Andrew Fusek Peters began storytelling in the 1980's. He has written and edited over 60 books for young people. His books include *The Barefoot Book of Strange and Spooky Stories, Roar! Bull! Roar!*, *Falcon's Fury* as well as the exciting thriller series *Skateboard Detectives*.

Usha Bahl
Usha Bahl is a multilingual teacher and a storyteller with a long experience of working in schools in London. She has been involved in promoting dual text stories acknowledging those who have bilingual skills.

Helen Frances
Helen Frances lives in Sheffield where she writes and tells stories. As a young adult she studied English and Icelandic literature. Since discovering the world of storytelling she has begun to explore the great folk traditions of the world and the wonderful effect the spoken word has on the listener.

Helen East

Helen East was born in Colombo but settled in London in 1979, where she started working as a storyteller. She has directed several major regional arts and storytelling projects. Since 2002 Helen has regularly led storywalks in Shropshire and the borders and in Kew Gardens, London. She has toured South America, telling stories in primary and secondary schools.

Jess Smith

Jess Smith grew up in Scotland. As a child she lived in a bus with her parents and seven sisters travelling around the country. Jess acquired storytelling skills from her elders. Her books include *Jessie's Journey*, *Tales From the Tent*, *Tears for a Tinker* and *Bruar's Rest*.